The World Around Us

BASED ON **TIMOTHY GOES TO SCHOOL** AND OTHER STORIES BY

ROSEMARY WELLS

ILLUSTRATED BY MICHAEL KOELSCH

PUFFIN BOOKS

Mrs. Jenkins's Class,

Mrs. JENKINS

TIMOTHY

FRITZ

YOKO

CHARLES

Hilltop School

DORIS

NORA

CLAUDE

FRANK

FRANK

"**TODAY** we're going to talk about a person you all know a lot about," says Mrs. Jenkins. "You!"

"Who?" asks Timothy. "Me?"

"Yes, Timothy," says Mrs. Jenkins. "You, and Charles, and Claude, and Doris, and everyone else in our class. What can you all tell me about yourselves?"

"I can play the violin," says Yoko.

"I like baseball," says Nora.

"I can write my name," says Fritz.

"Great!" says Mrs. Jenkins. "You are all very special. Now take out your crayons and draw a picture of yourself."

What is special about *you*? What do you know how to do?

The Next Step

Draw a picture of yourself on a big piece of paper. Ask an adult to help you write the following on your picture: your name, your age, your favorite color, your favorite food, your favorite toy, and your favorite thing to do.

5

TIMOTHY'S FAMILY

"There are all different kinds of families," Mrs. Jenkins tells the class. "Some are big and some are small. Who is in your family?"

"My parents are in my family," says Timothy.

"My family is my mother and me," says Yoko. "I have a lot of aunts, uncles, and cousins, too."

"My mom, dad, sister, and baby brother are in my family," says Nora.

Who are the people in your family? Who is the oldest person in your family? Who is the youngest person in your family?

YOKO'S FAMILY

Nora's Family Album

NORA, AGE 1

NORA, AGE 2, WITH DAD

NORA, MOM, JACK, DAD, KATE

 The Next Step

Make a family tent. Ask an adult to help you fold a piece of paper in half lengthwise. Draw a picture of your family on the bottom half. Now stand up your family tent!

"Families live in many different places," says Mrs. Jenkins. "But they all call the place they live the same thing—home. What can you tell me about your home?"

"I live in a yellow house," says Timothy.

"I live in an apartment building," says Yoko.

"My cousins live on a farm," says Fritz. "I visit them every summer."

"Good," says Mrs. Jenkins.

Look at the pictures of homes on the next page.

How are they the same? How are they different?

 The Next Step

Draw a picture of your own home. What color is it? Is it big or small? How many floors does it have? Do you know your address? Practice writing it.

House

Apartment building

Townhouse

Farm

9

"A community is a place where people live and work together," says Mrs. Jenkins. "There are communities all over the world, in big cities and in small towns. What are some places in your community?"

"There is a fire station," says Nora. "And there's a police station, too."

"There's a park," says Doris.

"And there's a grocery store," says Timothy.

Look at the picture of Timothy's community. Try to find each of these things in the picture: post office, police station, park, supermarket, and school. What other things do you see in Timothy's community?

 **The Next Step**

Are any of the things in Timothy's community in your community, too? Try to think of five different places in your community.

Firefighter   *Police officer*   *Mail carrier*

Mrs. Jenkins's class is taking a walk through town.

"Community helpers are people who keep our communities safe and clean," says Mrs. Jenkins. "Do you see any community helpers?"

"There's the crossing guard," says Charles. "He helps people cross the street safely."

"I see a mail carrier," says Claude. "She delivers letters and packages."

"Very good," says Mrs. Jenkins.

Look at the pictures above. What does each community helper do?

 The Next Step

Do you know any community helpers? What kind of work does each community helper that you know do?

HELPER	JOB	✓
TIMOTHY	JUICE	
NORA	LINE LEADER	⭐
FRITZ	BLOCKS	
CLAUDE	WATER PLANTS	⭐
YOKO	PAPER PASSER	
FRANKS	SNACKS	
CHARLES	ART HELPER	⭐
DORIS	ERASE BOARD	

"Just as community helpers work together to keep communities safe and clean," Mrs. Jenkins says, "you all work together to make our classroom a neat and happy place. What are some ways everyone helped today?"

"I passed out paint at art time," said Charles.

"I watered the plants," said Claude.

"When we lined up to go to music," said Nora, "I was the leader of the line."

"Wonderful," says Mrs. Jenkins. "It is important that everyone helps out."

Look at the picture and say how everyone is helping today.

 **The Next Step**

Do you have jobs in your classroom or at home? How do you help out?

"This is a map of the world," says Mrs. Jenkins. "It is a picture of the different continents in the world. There are seven continents. Who knows what ours is called?"

"I know," says Timothy. "We live in North America."

"Very good," says Mrs. Jenkins. "Does anyone know the names of any other continents?"

"Asia," says Yoko. "My grandparents live there."

"Europe," says Fritz. "My family went on vacation there once."

Look at the map. Can you find North America? Do you know the names of any other continents?

The Next Step

Look at a map of the United States. Do you know the name of the state you live in? Ask an adult to show you where your state is on the map. What other states do you know? Have you visited any other states?

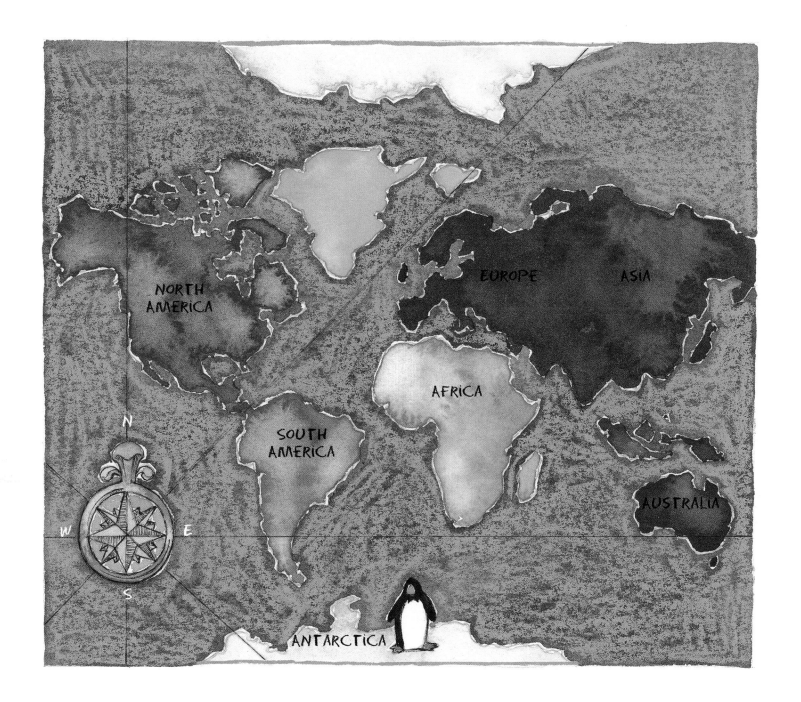

NORTH
AMERICA

EUROPE

ASIA

AFRICA

SOUTH
AMERICA

AUSTRALIA

N

W   E

S

ANTARCTICA

"People get from one place to another in many different ways," says Mrs. Jenkins.

"Can anyone name some?"

"Cars," says Claude. "And buses."

"Planes," says Fritz. "And trains."

"Very good!" says Mrs. Jenkins.

Look at the pictures below. Which are things used to get from one place to another?

The Next Step

Which of these have you used to get from one place to another: bicycle, car, bus, subway, train, plane, or boat? Which is your favorite?

"Every country has a special flag," Mrs. Jenkins tells the class. "Our flag has stars and stripes. Does anyone know what any flags from other countries look like?"

"The flag of Canada has a maple leaf in the middle," says Fritz.

"And Japan's flag has a big red circle on it," says Yoko.

"That's right," says Mrs. Jenkins. "Each country's flag is different."

Look at the pictures at the top of the page. Point to the flag of the United States. Point to the flag of Canada. Point to the flag of Japan.

 **The Next Step**

Look at a picture of the American flag. How many stripes do you see? How many stars do you see?

"Now we're going to talk about holidays," says Mrs. Jenkins. "A holiday is a special day for celebrating. People celebrate different holidays all over the world. Who can name a holiday?"

"I can," says Nora. "Thanksgiving."

"Very good," says Mrs. Jenkins. "That's when we give thanks for the things we have."

"The Fourth of July," says Fritz. "I love fireworks!"

"The Fourth of July is Independence Day," Mrs. Jenkins says. "On that day we celebrate our freedom."

What holiday does each picture on the next page make you think of?

The Next Step

What are some holidays you celebrate with your family? What is your favorite holiday? How do you celebrate it?

The school day is over! Timothy and his friends all have places to go and things to do. Look at the picture and try to answer these questions:

Who is going to dance class?

Who is going to a violin lesson?

Who is going to play baseball?

Who is going to read a book?

Who is going to play soccer?

How can you tell?

The Next Step

What do you like to do after school or on the weekends? Draw a picture of what you like to do for fun.

Letter to Parents and Educators

The early years are a dynamic and exciting time in a child's life, a time in which children acquire language, explore their environment, and begin to make sense of the world around them. In the preschool and kindergarten years parents and teachers have the joy of nurturing and promoting this continued learning and development. The books in the *Get Set for Kindergarten!* series are designed to help in this wonderful adventure.

The activities in this book were created to be developmentally appropriate and geared toward the interests and abilities of pre-kindergarten and kindergarten children. After each activity, a suggestion is made for "The Next Step," an extension of the skill being practiced. Some children may be ready to take the next step; others may need more time.

Social studies teaches children about their expanding world and the people in it. The activities in *The World Around Us* help children understand their place as members of a family, classroom, neighborhood, and broader community. As children grow, they develop skills in dealing with others. This book aims to be part of the learning process by introducing early social studies skills in a fun, accessible manner.

Throughout the early years, children need to be surrounded by language and learning and love. Those who nurture and educate young children give them a gift of immeasurable value that will sustain them throughout their lives.

John F. Savage, Ed.D.
Educational Consultant